The right to kill

Colin Terrell
Michael Terrell

First published in Great Britain by Axis Education Ltd.

ISBN 978-1-84618-203-7

Axis Education, PO Box 459
Shrewsbury, SY4 4WZ

Email: enquiries@axiseducation.co.uk
www.axiseducation.co.uk

The last thing Owen Mason saw before he died was the flash from the gun barrel. The last thing he heard was the bang of the gun.

Owen Mason never felt the bullets going through his chest. Or being slammed against the wall behind him. Lifeless when he hit it. Slowly sliding down the filthy wall. Leaving a wide trail of blood and bits of lung.

Only one person saw what happened.

Owen Mason's killer walked forward and looked down at the body.

The body did not move. Owen Mason just lay there. Eyes wide open. Staring up. Not moving.

The killer knew Owen Mason was dead.

The killer smiled at the body and walked away.

★★★★

PC Karen Cole was patrolling the Rose Hill Estate. Her radio clicked in.

'Cole. We've just had a call that there's a body in Rose Hill underpass. Get there as quick as you can. But wait for backup before going into the underpass.'

PC Cole answered, 'Okay. Message received. It'll take me about five minutes to get there. I'll wait for backup. Over and out.'

As she hurried through the estate she heard the distant sirens of backup cars.

Outside the underpass four armed police officers jumped out of the first car. All were wearing black bullet proof vests. Black helmets. And carrying black guns.

With their guns ready, the armed response officers inched into the underpass.

Detective Inspector Harry Baker pulled up in a second car. Cole and Baker knew each other.

As the DI got out of his car Cole asked, 'Why all the guns? I thought it was just a body. A druggie or something.'

'Not this one,' said DI Baker. 'Whoever called it in said they'd seen a body. The caller didn't leave a name. Said it looked like a shooting. Blood and guts all over the place.

We're not sure if the killer's still around. That's why the gun squad's here.'

Cole and the DI waited outside the underpass close to the cars.

Eventually, one of the armed response squad came out of the underpass. He beckoned Cole and Baker to come forward.

'Looks like it's all clear. This one's messy. We've called for the Crime Scene Investigation team. They're on their way.'

Cole and Baker went into the underpass. The body was half upright against a side wall slumped in a pool of blood. The head was hanging to the side. Bits of bone and guts spread around the body and on the wall.

PC Cole looked at the dead man's face.

'I know him,' she said. 'He's from the estate.'

'Know his name?' asked Baker.

'Owen Mason,' she said. 'I think he's about sixteen or seventeen. Looks older with those tattoos and shaved head.'

She paused for a moment before saying, 'He's into drugs. Small-time dealer I think. Nothing big. He's the leader of the Rose Hill Gang. Runs this estate like some kind of king.'

She pointed to the right arm of the body.
'See the tattoo? One of the gang thinks he's a
tattoo artist. It's supposed to be a rose
dripping blood with a knife through it. All the
gang members have one.'

Baker squatted down to look more closely at
the chest wound.

'Two shots I think,' he said. 'Looks like they
went right through his chest.'

He looked up at Cole. 'What do you think?
Reckon this might be a gang thing?'

Cole nodded, but didn't say anything.

'Not a lot more we can do,' said Baker, 'not till the crime scene team have finished.'

They walked back to Baker's car. As they left the underpass Cole pointed up at some phone wires. A pair of old trainers was hanging by its laces from the wires.

'Those trainers mark the border between two gangs,' she said. 'Bitter rivals they are. The Lee Street Gang and the Rose Hill Gang. There's lots of aggro between them. According to the Lee Street Gang, anybody in that underpass is on their turf.'

As she spoke, more sirens sounded and the CSI cars arrived.

★★★★

The next day PC Cole was asked to go to Harry Baker's office.

'You sent for me, sir?' she asked.

'Last night you said you knew some of the Rose Hill Gang,' he said.

PC Cole nodded.

'I've asked if you can work with my team for a few days,' said DI Baker, 'following up on last night's killing. Can you join in with the door to door enquiries around the estate? Ask if anybody knows anything. You know the drill.'

'Okay, I'll ask around,' she said. 'But don't expect much.'

'I know, I know,' said the DI, 'we won't get anything we can use. But you know how it is. We've got to look as if we're interested.' He hesitated before adding, 'Even if we don't give a toss about who shot him. Or why.'

PC Cole spent the day on the estate knocking on doors, asking questions.

She got nothing. Nobody had seen anything. Nobody knew anything. Late in the afternoon she looked at her watch. Half past four.

Behind her she heard a woman's voice call out, 'PC Cole.'

Turning around she recognised the woman at once.

'Hello, Mrs Ashley,' the policewoman replied. 'How's it going?'

'Oh, not so bad,' said Mrs Ashley. 'Haven't seen you in a long time, not since...'

Mrs Ashley couldn't finish the sentence.

PC Cole guessed what she was trying to say. 'We were all really sad when Alec died.'

She paused before adding, 'And hearing the cause of death too. I'm sorry. He was such a nice lad.'

Mrs Ashley's eyes were filled with tears.

'Well, I'm sure he's somewhere better than on this estate,' said Mrs Ashley. 'He wasn't happy in this life. Hated living here. What with always being called a spastic. And with his learning difficulties and all.'

Mrs Ashley pointed to a blue door further up the road. 'That's my place,' she said. 'Number ten, just there. If you've been here all day, perhaps you'd like a cup of tea?'

PC Cole was about to go off-duty but she was gasping for a drink. 'Yeah, that'd be great,' she said gratefully. 'I'm really knackered. It's near the end of my shift.'

Mrs Ashley searched in her handbag for a key. 'Are you asking questions about that killing yesterday? I hear it's Owen Mason that's dead.'

Mrs Ashley found her key and looked directly at PC Cole.

'Serves him right after what he did to Alec. A right nasty piece of work he was. And I could think of worse words to use.'

Mrs Ashley opened her front door. PC Cole sat at the kitchen table while the older woman made the tea.

'I don't suppose anybody's telling you much about Owen Mason,' said Mrs Ashley.

PC Cole took a sip of tea and nodded saying, 'No. Not a thing.'

'And nobody will tell you anything either,' said Mrs Ashley. 'Round here we're all terrified of that Rose Hill Gang. All of us. All the time.'

'After my Gary was killed in that accident, I don't know. How can I deal with these bullies?'

The poor woman, thought PC Cole.

She knew Mrs Ashley's husband, Gary, had

been killed in a motorway pile up two years ago. And last year her son died. Some people have rotten luck.

Not wanting to dwell on the past PC Cole asked, 'So the lads in the gang have been causing trouble again?'

'Lads you say? Well, people say they're only young,' said Mrs Ashley, 'but they don't look it. Not with all those tattoos and shaved heads. They may be only fifteen or sixteen,' she went on, 'but they always move around in a big gang. With their baseball caps and hoods you can't see their faces. Half of them are on drugs. Stealing things. Calling us names. Laughing at us.'

Mrs Ashley was getting more and more upset, but she couldn't stop.

'Remember what everybody said about how Alec died? Even you lot said he was just messing about on the side wall of that bridge across the railway line. You lot said it was an accident, but I know different.'

'The court decided it was an unfortunate accident,' PC Cole tried to comfort the woman.

'Accident?' Mrs Ashley nearly shouted, shaking her head angrily. 'That was no accident. I knew my Alec. Always scared of heights he was. And terrified of that Owen Mason. That thug had been bullying Alec since infant school. Alec was afraid to go out the door.'

'That Owen Mason,' Mrs Ashley went on between loud sobs, 'him and his mates were always shouting at Alec. "Look, there's the spazza. He still can't walk straight, dragging that gammy leg." That's what they said. You know they even said they'd cut Alec's leg off for him if he wanted.'

PC Cole said as softly as she could, 'I am sorry Mrs Ashley. But there were so many witnesses. They all said Alec got up on that wall beside the bridge by himself, for fun. Like he was playing about.'

By now Mrs Ashley was weeping so much

that she could hardly speak. But there was no stopping her.

'Witnesses?' she sobbed. 'All of them were in the Rose Hill Gang. And all mates of Owen Mason. Oh yeah, and all of them were on that bridge when Alec fell off the wall onto the railway line. That bloody Owen Mason and every single one of his gang said my Alec got up on that wall by himself. They even said they'd told Alec to be careful. That's a complete lie. I know exactly what happened. And I told them in the court. You were there. You heard me. But nobody listened.'

She wiped her eyes on the sleeve of her jumper.

'Alec stayed alive in the hospital for two days. I was with him the whole time. He was in a coma but he woke up just once. That's when he told me what really happened. He told me everything. Owen Mason had a knife. He'd forced Alec to get up on that side wall. He said he wanted to see if my Alec could balance on top of it with his gammy leg.'

'He was going to slash my Alec's face if he didn't walk on that wall. Right up there, above the railway line. My Alec was probably crying his eyes out when he climbed up.'

PC Cole shook her head and said, 'But there were so many witnesses who said different. We had to believe them. It was your word against all of them. They all said that Alec went on that wall just for a laugh. What could we do? We had to believe them.'

Mrs Ashley was still sobbing.

'Yeah right,' she said angrily, 'there were eleven other bloody witnesses. An' all members of that gang of hooligans. All sniggering and laughing outside the court like it was one big joke.'

'That Owen Mason was evil. Really evil. He's the one that killed my Alec. And afterwards he just kept laughing about it, winking at me every time I saw him.'

Mrs Ashley wiped her eyes again. 'I'm glad

that Mason is dead. Being shot was just too good for him. It was too quick for that... that... bastard! I wish he'd suffered real pain. He should have died slowly. He should have been made to feel as scared as he made my Alec feel.'

Mrs Ashley stopped talking. She just sat there. Head bowed. Sobbing.

There was a knock on the door.

PC Cole got up and said, 'You just sit there. I'll get it.'

At the door stood Mrs Ashley's two youngest children just home from school – a boy aged ten and a girl about seven. PC Cole followed them in to see their mother. Mrs Ashley turned away from them. Dabbing at her eyes. Trying to dry her tears.

When she turned around she tried to smile. 'Now both of you,' she said, 'go to the bathroom and get cleaned up.'

Trying to sound cheerful, Mrs Ashley added, 'And for getting home so quickly you can have some sweets. Where's my handbag?'

The bag was on the back of one of the chairs. Both children grabbed for it. They were in such a hurry that they knocked the bag to the floor. It dropped upside down and everything fell out.

PC Cole half got out of her chair to help but Mrs Ashley quickly pushed her back.

The widow bent down to scoop everything off the floor. She seemed frantic. Working as fast as she could, Mrs Ashley swooped to gather her things. Sweets. Keys. A powder compact. Lipstick. She stuffed them all back in her handbag.

PC Cole sat back down surprised she'd been shoved so quickly. And so hard.

But she'd seen enough. Before Mrs Ashley had time to thrust everything back in her handbag, PC Cole got just a quick glance. Less than a second. That's all. But she'd seen it.

Among the things on the floor was a handgun.

Mrs Ashley finally got everything back in her handbag. Flustered, she stood up and snapped the bag shut. Looking at PC Cole she said, 'I'd better go and get the kids cleaned up.'

Mrs Ashley clutched her handbag tightly to her chest with both arms wrapped around it.

The policewoman stood up from her chair. 'I'd better go as well,' she said. 'I need to get home. Thanks for the tea.'

★★★★

PC Cole headed down the road. She turned her head to speak into her radio. She needed to tell DI Baker what she'd seen.

She hesitated, then changed her mind. Switching off her radio the PC took out her notebook. Holding a pen, she was about to make some notes. Then she stopped to think.

How did Mrs Ashley know that Owen Mason had been shot? The police hadn't released that information. Only one person could possibly know – that had to be the killer. And what about the gun in Mrs Ashley's handbag?

PC Cole closed her notebook and walked to the patrol car with her mind racing. She listed her thoughts.

One scumbag dead.

One mother who might go to jail for life.

Two young kids left without a mother.

Thoughts tumbled around in her head. She stopped beside some rubbish bins and stayed still for a few minutes. Thinking. She made up her mind.

PC Cole said quietly to herself, 'This is going to be a gang land killing. Unsolved.'

★★★★